Who Sank the Boat?

To my mother
Esma Griffiths

Who Sank the Boat?

Pamela Allen

Puffin Books

Puffin Books

Penguin Books Australia Ltd

487 Maroondah Highway, PO Box 257

Ringwood, Victoria 3134, Australia

Penguin Books Ltd

Harmondsworth, Middlesex, England

Penguin Putnam Inc.

375 Hudson Street, New York, New York, 10014, USA

Penguin Books Canada Limited

10 Alcorn Avenue, Toronto, Ontario, Canada M4V 3B2

Penguin Books (N.Z.) Ltd

Cnr Rosedale and Airborne Roads, Albany, Auckland, New Zealand

Penguin Books (South Africa) (Pty) Ltd

4 Palinghurst Road, Parktown 2193, South Africa

First published in 1982 by Thomas Nelson in Australia

Published in Puffin, 1988

21 23 25 24 22 20

Offset from the Thomas Nelson edition

Made and printed in Hong Kong through Bookbuilders Ltd.

National Library of Australia
Cataloguing-in-Publication data:

Allen, Pamela
Who sank the boat?

ISBN 0 14 050940 2

1. Animals   Juvenile poetry. 2. Title

A821.3

Beside the sea, on Mr Peffer's place,
there lived

a cow, a donkey, a sheep, a pig,
and a tiny little mouse.

They were good friends,
and one warm sunny morning,
for no particular reason,
they decided to go
for a row in the bay.

Do you know who sank the boat?

Was it the cow
who almost fell in,
when she tilted the boat
and made such a din?

No, it wasn't the cow
who almost fell in.

Do you know who sank the boat?

Was it the donkey
who balanced her weight?
Who yelled,
'I'll get in at the bow before it's too late.'

No, it wasn't the donkey
who balanced her weight.

Do you know who sank the boat?

Was it the pig
as fat as butter,
who stepped in at the side
and caused a great flutter?

No, it wasn't the pig
as fat as butter.

Do you know who sank the boat?

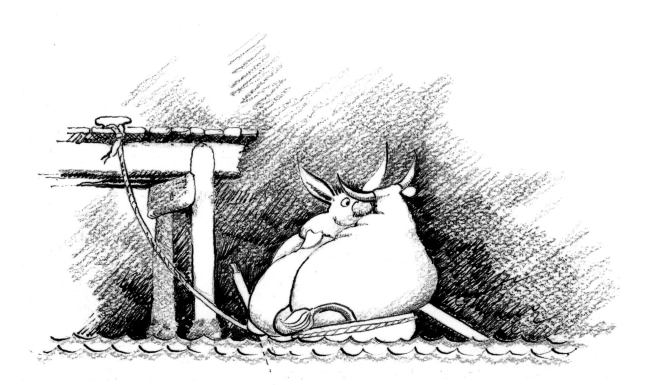

Was it the sheep
who knew where to sit
to level the boat
so that she could knit?

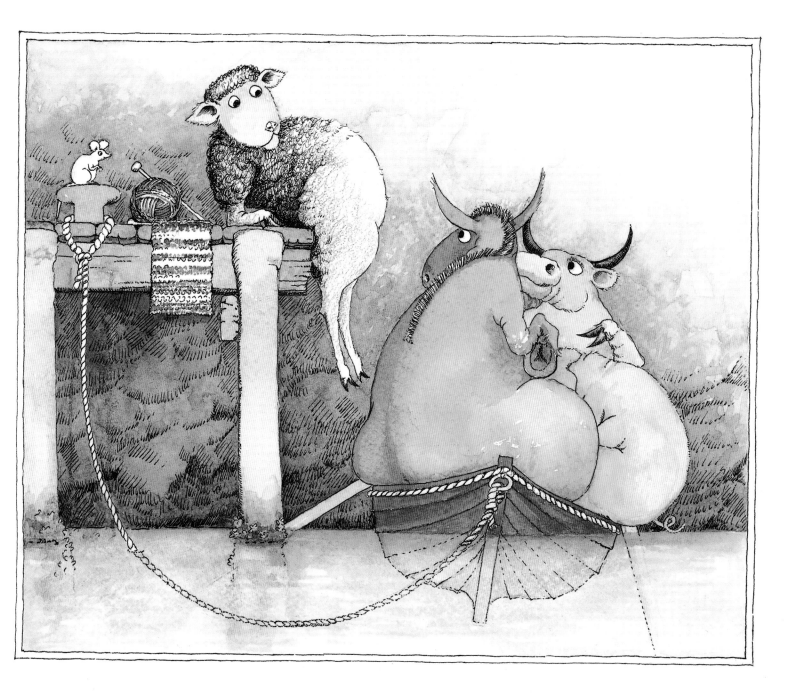

No, it wasn't the sheep
who knew where to sit.

Do you know who sank the boat?

Was it the little mouse,
the last to get in,
who was lightest of all?

Could it be him?

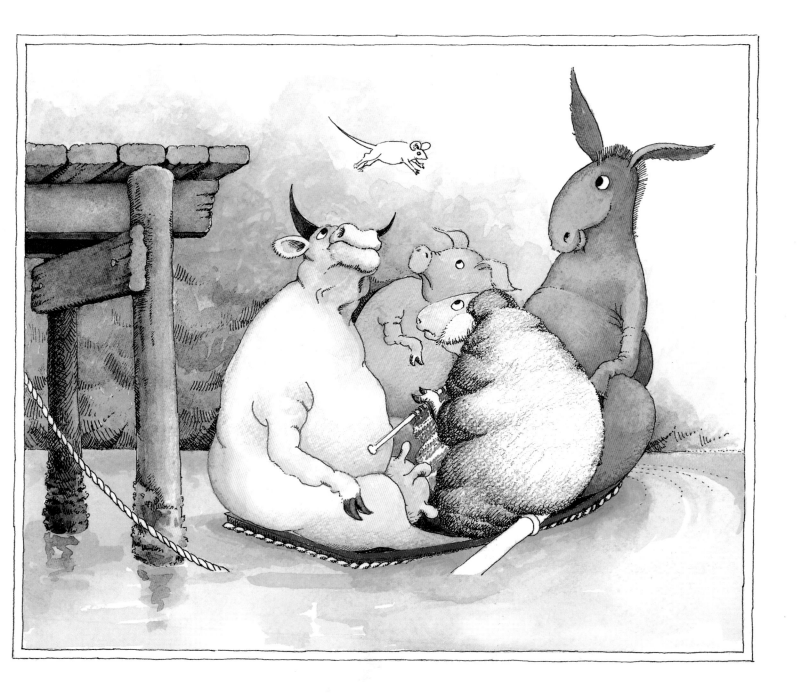

You DO know who sank the boat.